ALIEN ADVENTURES

3 STORIES IN ONE

Franzeska G. Ewart

Jamila Gavin

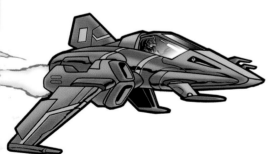

Sam McBratney

EGMONT

We bring stories to life

The Pen-Pal from Outer Space was first published in Great Britain 1998
Deadly Friend was first published in Great Britain 1994
Stranger From Somewhere in Time was first published in Great Britain 1994
Published in one volume as *Alien Adventures* 2008
by Egmont UK Limited
239 Kensington High Street
London W8 6SA

Text copyright © 1998 Franzeska G. Ewart; 1994 Jamila Gavin; 1994 Sam McBratney
Illustrations copyright © 1998 Simone Lia; 2000 Kev Hopgood; 2000 Martin and Ann Chatterton

The moral rights of the authors and illustrators have been asserted

ISBN 978 1 4052 4074 1

1 3 5 7 9 10 8 6 4 2

A CIP catalogue record for this title is available from the British Library

Printed and bound in Singapore

CONTENTS

The Pen-Pal from Outer Space
Franzeska G. Ewart

Deadly Friend
Jamila Gavin

Stranger From Somewhere in Time
Sam McBratney

Chapter One

IF THERE WAS one thing in the whole wide world that was the *worst* thing in the whole wide world it was being at a new school, Jasbir thought for the millionth time.

It wasn't that people didn't try. Mrs Hyslop, the teacher, tried very hard to make Jasbir feel welcome. On Jasbir's first day, Mrs Hyslop introduced her to all the other children and asked for a volunteer to look after her.

Mrs Hyslop chose Shahid. Shahid took his job very seriously and Jasbir listened politely as he gave her three conducted tours of the playground.

'Did you know,' he said as they walked, 'that some frogs lay their eggs on the female's back and the skin grows over them and then when the tadpoles hatch they have to eat their way out?'

Jasbir admitted that she had not known.

'And did you know that some spiders actually live underwater?' Shahid went on. 'They construct special webs, and trap enough air in them to enable them to live for many days. And talking about spiders, it is said that a spider can live for a year – yes, a year – without any food at all. Did you know that?'

By the end of the day Jasbir felt rather dizzy – partly because she had walked in circles and partly because she had shaken her head so much.

On the second morning, Mrs Hyslop chose the MacKenzie twins,

Rory and Gordon.

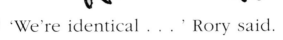

'We're identical . . . ' Rory said.

' . . . but I'm three minutes older,' Gordon finished.

'And we have a grandmother in Glenrothes,' Rory told her.

'And another grandmother in Dundee,' Gordon added.

'We also have a grandfather in Leicester,' Rory said.

'But he is not the husband of our Glenrothes granny . . .' Gordon pointed out.

'. . . or our Dundee granny,' Rory said.

'It's a tad confusing,' they both admitted, shaking their identical heads gravely.

On the third morning, Mrs Hyslop forgot to choose a person to look after Jasbir. Jasbir was secretly very relieved.

She *had* rather hoped that perhaps Mrs Hyslop would ask Aneesa. Aneesa sat right at the back of the class and was very quiet. Jasbir had never actually *spoken* to Aneesa, but she had seen her in the cloakroom on the first morning when she was looking for a place to hang her coat. Aneesa had given her such a lovely smile that Jasbir knew she was nice.

It had been a lovely rosy smile, but it had also been very shy. Since then, whenever they met, Aneesa seemed as though she would speak, and often Jasbir opened her mouth to say 'Hi' but somehow nothing happened. It was very sad.

One day Mrs Hyslop held up a large piece of paper.

'Primary Four,' she said, 'I have a surprise for you. I have got a list of pen-pals – from all over the world. Now listen carefully, and you can each choose one to write back to.'

There was silence as everyone listened carefully.

Jasbir nearly put her hand up for Tanya from America because she had a horse and wanted to be Miss America when she grew up, but then she changed her mind.

Then she nearly went for Hiroko from Japan, but decided against it when she heard she kept crickets as pets.

'Right – last one,' Mrs Hyslop said suddenly. 'This is Franz from Germany. It says, "I study English since two years now and I seek much practice. I love difficult sums."

So – who is going to take Franz?'

Jasbir's heart sank. She wished she had chosen Hiroko, despite the crickets. She put up her hand. Then she heard Mrs Hyslop say, 'Fine, James – I am sure you will give Franz lots of very good practice. You'll have to remember your full stops and capitals though, and learn your four times table.'

Jasbir looked round to see James taking a note of Franz's name, and then she looked back at Mrs Hyslop.

'Oh, Jasbir,' Mrs Hyslop gasped, 'I am sorry! I haven't got a pen-pal for you! It's with you being new. I'll get you one, of course, but it will take a few weeks – sorry. Would you like to read a book for now?'

So Jasbir went to the library corner while everyone else began their letters. She chose a book but she didn't feel like reading. She tried to comfort herself with the thought that she would get a pen-pal eventually, but it didn't help.

After break, as she trailed sadly back to the library corner, Jasbir noticed a piece of paper lying on her desk. She picked it up.

No one was watching her, so she sat down to read it. As she read, her mouth opened wider and wider and her heart beat faster and faster.

Jasbir *did* have a pen-pal. A very strange pen-pal indeed.

hasn't got as many fingers as I have.
That's because we Zargons grow more and more
fingers the older we get. There are some very old
Zargons who have over fifty fingers on each hand.
It makes us terribly
good at sums.
Are you good at sums?
I also have a pet,
and this is it:
We call it Blippo and
we control it from a box.
Please write back. Leave your letter on the
third shelf of the teacher's cupboard, beside the
chalk, and I will cause it to rematerialise
on Zargos. As we say in Zargon — be
happy, and may everyone you meet make you
want to stick your fingers in your ears.

ZipPy*

Jasbir folded up ZipPy*'s letter and put it in her bag. She knew exactly what she would do. Maths had been the biggest nightmare since she joined the new school. Somehow, she just couldn't get the hang of it and maths tests were the worst. Jasbir pictured ZipPy* with all his fingers, and she smiled.

She would ask ZipPy* to use his superior powers to help her with the maths test.

When the bell rang, Jasbir was the first out of the classroom. She ran home, shut herself in her bedroom and slowly, carefully, she began to write:

Dear ZipPy*,

I am very happy to have you as my pen-pal.

I will tell you all about myself, but first there

is a little matter of a maths test I would like

to discuss. . .

14

Chapter Three

IT WAS INCREDIBLY dusty on the third shelf
beside the chalk.

Jasbir waited till everyone had gone out,
then headed for the teacher's cupboard with
her letter.

She had spent a long time the night before
composing it. She had told ZipPy* all about
her family – she too had a little 'bother' and
she had tried hard to draw Pritpal so that
ZipPy* should really know what he looked
like.

At the end of the letter, just in case ZipPy*
might forget, Jasbir had written:

P.S. Please don't forget about the maths test.

I would be most grateful for any help at all - I am

hopeless at maths, probably because I've only got

ten fingers.

For the rest of the morning Jasbir could
concentrate on nothing. Her eyes kept going
to the cupboard as though she expected to
see her letter floating
out and up to the planet
Zargos, but nothing
happened.

After lunch it was time for the maths test – and still nothing. Jasbir put her hand up.

'Mrs Hyslop,' she said, and Mrs Hyslop looked at her in surprise.

'Can I get some more chalk for you? There's none left.'

Mrs Hyslop looked rather puzzled. 'Isn't there?' she said. 'Oh very well, thank you, Jasbir.'

Jasbir rushed to the cupboard. She felt along the third shelf . . . and, yes! There *was* a reply! Her own letter had gone, and in its place there was just one very small piece of paper.

Jasbir took out two long pieces of blue chalk and

17

the paper and hurried back to her seat.

'Right, Jasbir – are you ready?' Mrs Hyslop said, and Jasbir nodded.

'Good,' Mrs Hyslop sighed. 'Now – I have six teams of boys, and there are four boys in each team, how many boys is that altogether?'

Jasbir felt the usual sickening feeling in her stomach. Carefully, so no one would see, she uncrumpled the piece of paper from Planet Zargos. It said:

Of course I will help you with your maths test – nothing simpler! Just remember – altogether means add or multiply. That's important. The other important thing is – keep calm, and I will be with you.

Be happy, and M. E. Y. M. M. Y. W. T. S. Y. F. I. Y. E.

Chapter Four

AFTER SCHOOL, MRS Hyslop asked Jasbir to
stay behind.

'What an improvement in your maths,
Jasbir,' she said. 'You deserve a gold star! Oh
dear me,' she went on, 'why does this drawer
get into such a mess? Ah! Here it is,' she said
at last, fishing a pastille tin out from under a
mass of rubber bands and confiscated toys.

She opened it and sighed.

'None left! My, what a good class I have –
they go through gold stars so quickly. Run

and get me another packet out of the cupboard please, Jasbir.'

The stars were on the second shelf, but as Jasbir was used to looking on the third shelf beside the chalk she checked there too.

And to her utter amazement, she saw a new letter! She gave the stars to Mrs Hyslop and then she rushed home to read it.

Dear Jasbir,

Thank you so much for your letter. I loved hearing about your family. Today I am going to tell you about an adventure I once had. One day I was taking my pet Blippo for a walk when I heard a noise coming from the top of an Ognam tree. When I looked up, all I saw were five terrible red eyes staring back at me. As soon as I saw the eyes, I knew I was looking at a terrible two-mouthed purple Hooley! Hooleys can freeze you into ice, you know, and lick you with their two awful tongues until in the end . . . you disappear!

'Hoooo! Hoooo! Hoooo!' it went.

Then it stopped.

I waited and waited, but nothing happened. At last I
could not bear it any longer. I had to move. I looked
up at the Hooley, and do you know what it was
doing, Jasbir? It was laughing! And then I saw why.
It was watching Blippo, and Blippo was turning
somersaults faster and faster.

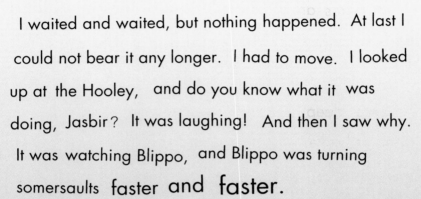

Now, I don't know if I explained but Blippo, my pet,
is not actually alive. If you saw Blippo's inside, he's

just wires and fuses and little lights and switches.

That means that, although he has got feelings of a

sort, he doesn't really belong to anyone. So I took

a big deep breath and,

in as brave

a voice as

I could manage

I said to the Hooley,

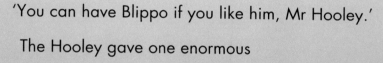

'You can have Blippo if you like him, Mr Hooley.'

The Hooley gave one enormous

'Hooo!' reached

down and lifted Blippo ever so

gently into the Ognam

tree and off it went.

I hope you like my adventure story and I am really looking forward to hearing yours. Write soon. Be happy, and may everyone you meet make you want to stick your fingers in your ears,

ZipPy*
X X X X X

Chapter Five

JASBIR SAT ON her bed and thought.
Compared to ZipPy*'s wonderful adventure
with the Hooley, nothing that had happened
to her seemed remotely interesting. What
could she write? She wasn't good at stories at
the best of times.

At school the next morning, Mrs Hyslop
said, 'Do you remember how the little boy in
your reading book loved to listen to his
grandpa's stories? Well, this morning you are

going to write your own story, like Grandpa's.
Make it as exciting as you can.'

So Jasbir sat, as she had the night before,
and thought and thought about what she
could write. She was staring at the blank
sheet of paper when suddenly a strange thing
happened.

Just like the day before in the maths test,
Jasbir felt a warm, rosy glow
inside and she pictured ZipPy*'s
face looking at her across
space. And she knew that
there was someone who
really wanted to hear
about her adventures.

Happily, Jasbir began to write:

My Adventure with Green Paint

Once upon a time when I was about four and a half we lived in a house near Manchester.

It was a new house, and the houses next door were not even finished.

One day I took my little brother, Pritpal, to see them. Pritpal was only two.

Outside the houses we found some tins of paint. It was green paint that the workmen were using to paint the doors. They had left the lid off one of the tins.

They had also left their brushes.

I took a brush and I dipped it in the paint. Then I painted big strokes of green on the wall. It looked lovely!

Then Pritpal wanted a paintbrush too. I gave him one and dipped it in the green paint for him.

Well, I was only four and a half – and after all the workmen should never have left the paint tin with its lid off.

Then . . . I decided to paint Pritpal.

At first he thought it was funny. Then he began to cry, so I took him home.

He was so sticky, I made him walk. I didn't fancy carrying him. Then the worst thing of all happened.

Pritpal was screaming so hard, Mum heard

him and came running out of the house.

She was wearing a beautiful pale pink
cardigan that my auntie had just knitted for
her. It was all covered in little sequins, and it
had taken my auntie months to knit.

Mum was so upset to see Pritpal crying, she
held out her arms and said, 'There, there,
Pritpal sweetie – whatever has happened to
you?'

And Pritpal threw himself into Mum's arms and rubbed his face all over her beautiful pale pink cardigan . . .

When Mum got over the shock of seeing Pritpal covered in green paint, she was very angry with me!

Pritpal and I had to be scrubbed and scrubbed, and I had to have my hair washed with turpentine. And the beautiful pale pink cardigan with the sequins . . .  had to be thrown in the bin!

Mrs Hyslop read the story. 'This is wonderful, Jasbir!' she said. 'It's worth at least three gold stars.'

She let Jasbir stay in at break to copy the story out – and when she wasn't looking, Jasbir slipped the first copy triumphantly onto the third shelf of the cupboard.

Chapter Six

FOR THE NEXT few weeks Jasbir and ZipPy*
went on exchanging letters till Jasbir felt that
she knew almost all there was to know about
him. But as the summer holidays got nearer
Jasbir began to feel very sad. How could she
send letters to ZipPy* if she couldn't put them
on the third shelf of the cupboard?

Then an idea came to her and she wrote to
ZipPy*.

Dear ZipPy*,

Thank you for your last letter. 'Zango'
sounds a marvellous game. I will suggest it to
Mrs Hyslop next time we are at the gym.
ZipPy*, I am going to ask you for a big favour,
and I hope you won't mind. You know how one
of your superior powers is reading brain waves?
Well, I was wondering whether
you could perhaps get inside
the brain waves of a
girl in my class. Her name is Aneesa. I would
just love to be her friend, you see.

I mean, it's great

having you, and I hope we'll

be pen-pals for ever and ever, but it's a long
summer without the teacher's cupboard,
and it would be so nice to have an Earth friend
to really do things with.
Could you manage to get inside Aneesa's head
and tell her that I think she's the
nicest person in the class
and I want to be her friend?
Please write soon.
Be happy, and may everyone you meet make
you want to stick your fingers in your ears.

Jasbir

Chapter Seven

THE NEXT DAY at school, Jasbir kept looking at Aneesa to see if ZipPy* had contacted her, but Aneesa just got on with her work as usual.

However, in the afternoon two very odd things happened that made Jasbir feel puzzled. Slowly she began to realise that everything was not as it seemed.

The first was during Spelling. Jasbir heard Mrs Hyslop talking to Aneesa.

'Now really, Aneesa – I don't expect such

carelessness from you! Look at the way you
have spelt "brother" – you have missed out
the "r" not once but every time. Now, rub out
each "bother" and write it properly –
BROTHER.'

Jasbir sucked the end of her pencil and
frowned. ZipPy* always spelt 'brother' as
'bother'. Jasbir had thought it was a Zargon
joke.

After playtime, a second odd
thing happened. Jasbir
heard Mrs Hyslop talking
angrily to Aneesa.

'Oh, Aneesa – what a
terrible mess all over
your work! It's covered
in blue chalky fingerprints! What have you
been up to, Aneesa?'

Spelling 'brother' as 'bother'? Jasbir thought.
Covered in blue chalkdust? There was
something very fishy going on – but surely
not? Surely not Aneesa, of all people?

Jasbir tiptoed to the cupboard and reached
up to the third shelf for the message she
knew would be there.

It was written on a very small piece of
paper, and it said:

Meet me behind the bike shed after school,

ZipPy*

When the bell rang, Jasbir rushed out. As she ran to the bicycle shed, there was a tiny part of her that did expect to see ZipPy* standing there. But another part of her knew that ZipPy* would not be there, and that in fact, ZipPy* would never write to her again.

And of course she was right. For, standing behind the bicycle shed was someone who, in the end, would be an even better friend than ZipPy* had been.

Jasbir stopped running. Aneesa turned to face her and began to walk slowly towards her, a large smile spreading across her face.

Then, at just the same time, both girls stopped and smiled at one another as they stuck their fingers in their ears and they both stood together in the rosy pinkness of Planet Zargos.

JAMILA GAVIN

ILLUSTRATED BY KEV HOPGOOD

To Heather, Louis and Rory

K.H.

The New Boy

'CHILDREN, MEET ADAM Starbright!'

The children gawped and giggled as their teacher frowned disapprovingly at their bad manners.

Adam Starbright stood stiffly at Mrs Walker's side. He was a bit like a dummy standing in the window of a clothing store. His face was as still as plastic and his eyes were the colour of water. His clothes were odd too. Mohun wondered where he had bought them. Not in Colston, that's for sure. You couldn't get anything worth wearing in Colston, except pants and vests and grannies' underwear. The clothes Adam Starbright

was wearing were similar to the grey and maroon
uniform they all wore, yet somehow different.
They were smooth and tight fitting, as though
his body had been poured into them.

Adam stared at Mohun. The new boy's eyes gazed steadily into his without blinking. Mohun stared back. He couldn't help it. It was as if Adam's gaze was a trap which had caught him and wouldn't let him go.

At that moment Gary Williams hissed across to Stephen Pitts, 'Adam Starbright! What a silly name. Do you think he goes twinkle twinkle in the dark!'

A ripple of sniggers swept around the room, as others repeated the joke.

Mohun, who still looked at Adam, heard the joke but didn't laugh. He remembered his own first day at school a year ago, when everyone had laughed at his name.

Although he had plenty of friends now, Mohun would always remember that day with a shudder. Adam didn't join in the laughter. He just gazed steadily at Mohun, as if he knew that Mohun too had been through the same experience and understood. They would be friends.

The sniggers rose louder, then stopped abruptly as Mrs Walker shouted above the hubbub.

'Children! Please!' Then she turned to Adam and said, 'I want you to sit over at that table between Mohun and Natasha. Go as quickly as possible.'

Adam went at once, in a straight line, across the tables, leaping on to the first and then striding across the tops to the next and the next until he arrived in his place.

'Well, REALLY!' exclaimed Mrs Walker breathlessly. 'What DO you think you're doing?'

'I calculated that the route I took to my desk was quickest by one point three and a half metres. Would you like me to show you my calculations?' asked Adam. 'You required me to go to my place as quickly as possible. So I did.'

'Adam! . . .' Mrs Walker began angrily. Then she stopped. He wasn't being insolent. He meant it. She paused, to give herself time to think, then she said, 'In future, NEVER on any account, step ON or OVER the tables. Tables are not for walking over. They are for sitting AT. Do you understand?'

'Yes, Mrs Walker,' replied the boy. 'I will not forget.'

'Now then, everybody, get out your English notebooks. I want you to write about your best friend.'

Mohun and Simon Boston grinned at each other across the room. They were best friends.

They would write about each other. There was
a rattle of drawers opening, as everyone pulled
out exercise books and snatched up pencils.
Out of the corner of his eye, Mohun had the
impression that Adam didn't open his drawer.
The boy's hand went straight through the table
top, as if it were water, and came out holding
his book. Mohun opened his mouth to exclaim,
but Adam caught his eye with a smile, slowly
twisting a pencil in his fingers. Then in a strange,

printy handwriting, moving to the right and back again to the left across the page like a computer printout, Adam wrote, 'My best friend is Mohun Banerjee.'

At break, Mohun, Simon and the others rushed out into the playground. Adam stood alone as the classroom emptied.

'Hurry out and play,' Mrs Walker urged him kindly as she collected up the exercise books. She nodded towards the playground, which they could see through the windows. Then she strode from the classroom, expecting Adam to follow. Out in the corridor, she turned to ask him whether he had brought a packed lunch, but he had vanished.

'Adam?' She looked back inside the classroom. There was no sign of him. 'Adam?'

Out in the playground, Adam raced towards Mohun and, with a flying leap, caught the football which Mohun had just kicked to Simon.

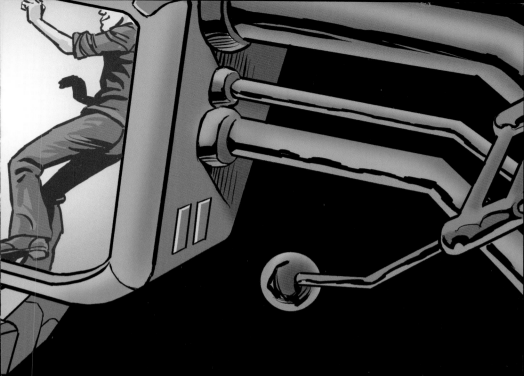

The Information Gatherers

'OH DEAR!' INFORMATION Gatherer 6 hissed through his teeth. 'I forgot.'

'What did you forget?' asked Mater, leaning over his shoulder and staring at the television screen. IG6 had zoomed into a closeup of Adam and Mohun side by side. Mater smiled with satisfaction. She couldn't help feeling a sense of pride at the way in which they had adapted Adam to the planet Earth. You could hardly tell that he was any different from the other children.

'I forgot to inform him about doors,' said IG6. 'He should have gone out through the door not through the wall. Humans have not yet learned how to break up into molecules. They still have to create spaces through which to pass, such as doorways and corridors.'

'That's the third error you've made today, IG6,' muttered Mater.

'Yes . . . yes . . . I'm not used to the slow speed with which they move on Earth.'

IG6 shook his head with wonder. 'But Adam has done well. He has carried out another task and now knows what a *school* is. He is following his instructions with credit.'

For two thousand years, the Information Gatherers had been exploring space. They had been searching for a planet with life on it.

Then they found Earth. Mater still shivered with the excitement of the discovery. Plans were made to send out research teams. How proud she was when her son, Adam, was chosen to join the team and gather information about life as a human child.

'Now he is investigating something called a *friend*. Do you think this human child is a *friend*?'

Mater and IG6 looked with interest as Adam kicked the ball to Simon.

The New Game

'ARE YOU COMING skateboarding after school?' asked Simon.

'No . . . I . . . ' Mohun hesitated, struggling briefly with himself.

'Go on!' urged Simon. 'I've got some new tricks to show you!'

'Simon, I've reached level nineteen in my new computer game. I must go on . . . don't you see?' Mohun tried to explain, longing to share his excitement with his best friend.

But Simon's voice was flat with disappointment. 'You never used to be like this,' he said.

'I've only got one more level to go and then I reach the Ultimate Destination and claim the prize.'

'What sort of prize?' asked Simon, slightly more interested.

'I don't know. It's a surprise.'

It had all started one day when the postman delivered a small brown packet to Mohun's house.

'It's for you,' Dad had said, tossing it to his son.

Mohun had ripped off the paper with excitement. Inside was a computer disc without a name. He rushed up to his room and slotted it in. Up on the screen came a title: 'Ultimate Destination'. A brief note told him that he had been selected to receive this computer game free, and that if he achieved the Ultimate Destination, he would get a fantastic prize.

The game was to help Information Gatherers from another planet who were travelling through space. They were collecting knowledge about star systems and sending it back to their base. Mohun had to blast away space pirates and dodge their way through rock storms; he had to rescue them from the magnetic pull of black holes and guide them from one planet to another, fighting off alien monsters and deadly microbes. At each step, he had to gather information and then move on to the next level of the game. It wasn't quite clear what or where the Ultimate Destination was. The instructions told him that he would know when he got there.

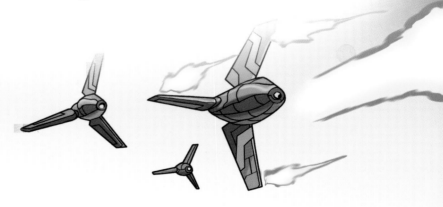

That was weeks ago, and ever since the disc arrived, Mohun had been playing it every spare moment. His mother got very upset with him.

'That game's taken over you,' she wailed. 'You don't care about anybody any more, not even Simon and he's your best friend! He used to be round here every day, now I haven't seen him for weeks. You don't eat, you don't sleep. You think of nothing but that machine. I feel like unplugging it!'

Mohun was horrified.

'Mum, don't. Don't ever touch my computer. It's taken me weeks to get to level eighteen. I've only another two levels to go and then I reach the Ultimate Destination. I'd die if you wiped the game or set me back to the beginning. Do you realise, I'd DIE'

Now he had reached level nineteen. Only one more level to go. The Information Gatherers had found a planet with life. A message appeared on the screen.

'MOHUN. DON'T GIVE UP. YOU ARE NEAR TO THE ULTIMATE DESTINATION.'

Virtual Reality

'YOU DID WELL today, Adam!' Mater appeared
before him.

On the new housing estate at the bottom of
the road, the Information Gatherers had created
Adam a house in Virtual Reality; a house which
was not real to anyone else except Adam. No
one else could see it, because no one else had
the special sensitive suit which covered his
whole body like a skin.

They had created a house such as humans lived
in. They wanted to understand everything about the
human way of life. So Adam now sat on a comfy
sofa watching television, with a plate of Marmite
sandwiches at his side and a mug of hot chocolate
in his hand.

'Mater!' protested Adam, as his mother appeared
on the living room carpet, interrupting his TV

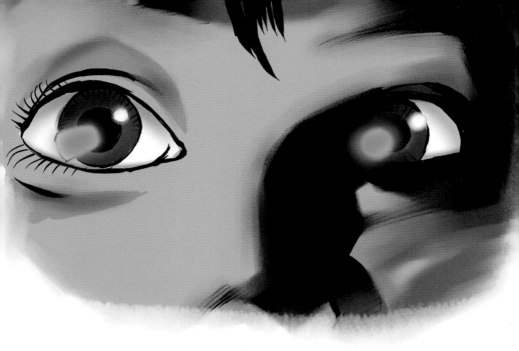

Friend or not?

MOHUN STARED AT the computer screen. In this last level, the game had changed. Now, he wasn't just firing rockets and lasers at attacking alien forces, he was being asked to exterminate an enemy here on Earth. But first he had to identify the enemy by asking questions.

Mohun tapped away and soon constructed an indentikit on the screen. Excitedly, he built up a description. The boy was one metre, six centimetres tall; white-skinned with blue eyes and fair hair; hobbies: football and skateboarding . . .

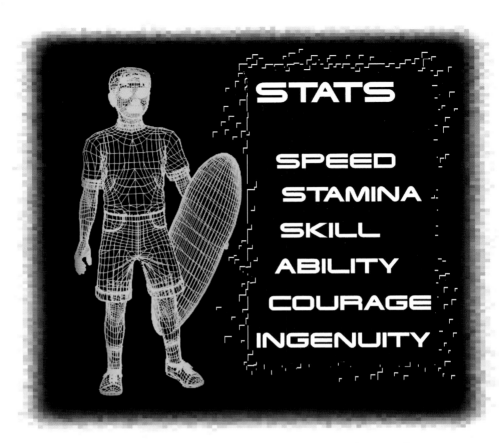

STATS

SPEED
STAMINA
SKILL
ABILITY
COURAGE
INGENUITY

A figure began to appear. It was a boy, about his age. He was skateboarding with a large group of other boys.

Mohun felt uneasy. He knew it was only a game, but . . . this looked real. Instead of space monsters, was he being asked to exterminate humans? Slowly, he took up the control pad. Reluctantly his thumbs hovered over the trigger, ready to fire.

The camera zoomed in closer to one of the boys. He was moving fast on his skateboard. It tracked quickly to keep up with him. The boy twisted and whirled round. The boy reached a slope and hurtled down, spinning in the air and landing perfectly at the bottom. He turned and threw up his arms in a gesture of triumph.

The camera came right into close-up.

'THIS IS YOUR ENEMY,' said the words beneath the picture.

It was Simon.

Mohun's hand jerked with the shock as he fired automatically, then he fell away from the computer in horror.

'That was my friend,' he screamed. 'That was my friend.'

He stumbled out of the room and down the stairs. He was running now. Running for all he was worth. He raced towards the park. He ran without stopping until he reached the gates, then the paved area around the pavilion and the slope on which all the skateboarders liked to practise. A crowd of people stood in a tight cluster. No one was skateboarding; they were all looking down at someone.

'There's been an accident,' someone said. 'Blooming skateboarders. A right menace they are.'

Mohun pushed through to the front. 'Simon?' he shouted desperately. It wasn't Simon. Mohun felt relief sweeping through him. Another boy lay curled up on the ground. Simon bent over him with concern.

'What happened?' asked Mohun in a shaky voice.

'The skateboard just flipped under me!' whispered Simon. 'But I don't understand it. I had already stopped. Something seemed to strike my skateboard and make me crash into Kevin.'

'Simon, I'm sorry!' stammered Mohun.

'Why?' asked Simon, puzzled. 'How can it be your fault?'

An ambulance came. The ambulance men checked Kevin carefully.

'No damage done that I can see,' said one of them cheerfully, 'but we'll take him off for an X-ray just in case,' and Kevin was whisked away.

As the crowds dispersed, Mohun suddenly saw Adam Starbright. Was it the late afternoon sun which seemed to make his body shimmer? He was by a tree at a distance. His eyes gleamed like metal balls.

They looked at each other. Mohun heard Adam's voice in his head saying, 'It's a pity you missed.'

Mohun frowned. 'Missed what?'

'The enemy,' said Adam and smiled.

Mohun felt a strange chill come over him.

'You can leave it to me, if you like,' came Adam's voice. 'I wouldn't want you to fail getting to your Ultimate Destination.'

Mohun shuddered. 'I've got to go!'

'Where are you going?' cried Simon, trying to grab Mohun's arm. 'What about me!' But Mohun had gone.

The Deadly Game

AT HOME MOHUN stared at the screen. It was different. Now it was laid out like a maze. Standing at the top left-hand entrance to the maze was a menacing figure in red.

He was the Annihilator, with a deadly weapon in his hand. He waited for Mohun to take up the control pad and move him towards the target. The target was in the very middle of the maze. It was Simon!

Mohun stared desperately at the screen. Simon was skateboarding home; sometimes picking up his skateboard to walk over grass or to cross a road, but then jumping on to it again, when there was a clear hard space.

'Welcome back to the game, Mohun.' The words appeared on the screen.

Mohun sat down.

'Do you still wish to reach Ultimate Destination and claim your prize?' asked the computer.

For weeks Mohun's whole aim had been to get to Ultimate destination. Now everything had changed. He seemed to be playing a deadly game, in which the last obstacle to his success was Simon. Simon was the final target and unless he eliminated him, he would never gain the prize.

Before, every time the computer had asked him, 'Do you wish to reach Ultimate Destination?' Mohun had pressed 'Y' for Yes. But now as he stared fearfully at his friend, innocently skateboarding home, Mohun tapped 'N' for No.

Suddenly a purple figure appeared in the bottom right-hand corner of the screen. It was another Annihilator. Someone else was controlling it. It moved quickly through the maze getting nearer and nearer to Simon.

Mohun leapt to his feet, and ran to the door.
His first instinct was to warn Simon. Then he
stopped. The Purple Annihilator was moving
ever nearer. Mohun knew he would never
reach Simon in time, and even if he did, how
could they escape the Annihilator?

He returned to his chair. He tapped in a
message: 'I wish to play the game.'

He grabbed the control pad as the computer said, 'Play.'

He pressed the button. His Red Annihilator moved from its top left corner. Mohun had control again. As the Purple Annihilator advanced from the right, Mohun's thumb hammered away. He guided his Red Annihilator through the maze towards Simon.

Simon had reached the top of his road. He had the strangest feeling that he was being followed. He looked behind him. A purple figure turned the corner and was catching up with him. Ahead of him he saw another figure all in red, coming towards him.

Simon got off his skateboard. He felt afraid.

Simon stood frozen to the spot in a state of shock. His skateboard lay in the gutter where it had rolled. Behind him Mohun was racing up the road. Before him stood Adam Starbright.

Mohun came and stood next to his friend. He put his arm around Simon's shoulders.

'Did you finish your game?' asked Simon.

'Yes.'

'What was the prize?'

'You,' said Mohun. 'Come on. Let's go.' Simon picked up the skateboard.

'Mohun!' Adam called out, His voice sounded crackly, like a radio wave. 'I only wanted you to be my friend.'

'You don't make friends by making enemies,' replied Mohun, and he and Simon turned away, walking side by side towards home.

Going Home

'THERE ARE THINGS about humans which we do not yet understand,' murmured IG6.

He and Mater studied the screen before them. 'We need more information. Our knowledge about humans is incomplete. We do not understand the meaning of *friend*.'

Mater looked it up in the dictionary again. '"*Friend*: a person whom one knows well and is *fond* of,"' she read out loud.

'And what is *fond*?' asked IG6.

'"*Fond*: having a liking for someone or something,"' read Mater. '"Tender and affectionate." We must instruct Adam.'

IG6 and Mater looked at the screen. Adam stood alone in the empty street.

'Bring him home,' Mater said.

Adam looked up into the sky. How lonely space was. The first evening star glimmered as his body melted and disintegrated into millions of molecules.

Sam McBratney

STRANGER FROM SOMEWHERE IN TIME

Illustrated by Martin and Ann Chatterton

My name is Helen.

Lorna is my friend. Her mum's a teacher and her dad was in the Army in Hong Kong, so she can count up to ten in Chinese.

Then there's Bopper, who can hardly count up to ten in English. His schoolbag is like a hospital for injured books and biros.

Murdo, the youngest, is round and gentle; he was upset for days when Mrs Fairley told him to sing quietly.

Finally there's Alan Ward, the best reader in our class. Everybody calls him Foxy. His head is full of things like time travel and computer games. You can be sure that he saves Planet Earth at least once a night from baddies like the Mad Wizard of the Universe.

'Ten thousand years,' said Foxy as we passed our brand-new shopping centre. 'That's a long time, you know. Maybe the Daleks will have wiped us out by then.'

'Exterminate, exterminate!' screamed Bopper, pointing his Dalek feelers at two ladies coming out of the shopping centre. They gave him a dirty look and walked on, unexterminated.

'Let's meet in Murdo's garage after tea,' said Foxy. 'We'll make our own time capsule. If everybody brings along something to bury, we can send a message into the future.'

I looked at Lorna to see if she thought this was a good idea. She did.

'Listen, Foxy,' I said, 'there's nothing in my house that I can bury for ten thousand years.'

He smiled patiently, as if my poor brain didn't understand how these things worked.

'We only have to bury the capsule for one night,' he said. 'We'll dig it up again in the morning. Look, I'll explain after tea, OK?'

They should have taken my advice, of course, but they didn't. It was four-to-one against me. And I hadn't a clue what to bring along for the Great Burying Ceremony!

Chapter Two

I ARRIVED IN Murdo's garage with a jar of anti-wrinkle cream borrowed from my mum, a can of de-icer borrowed from Dad, and a slinky toy that used to be able to go down the stairs on its own.

Lorna had brought along sunglasses, a Mickey Mouse toothbrush, an electric plug and an X-ray of the bone she'd broken last year. And a red Frisbee.

Foxy Ward produced a tin-opener, a pocket
calculator, a packet of sweetpea seeds, a
magnifying glass and a whistle. Since this whole
crazy idea came from him he also supplied the
time capsule – a white polystyrene box.

'My turn!' announced Bopper, laying a

chewed-up old shoe on the garage bench,
and then a round of brown bread. Next came
a disposable nappy, £400 of Monopoly money,
and a dead daddy-long-legs. Nobody said a
word as Foxy placed that little lot into the time
capsule. We were all speechless.

Now it was Murdo's turn. He'd only managed to think of two things. One was an oven glove and the other was a parcel wrapped in bright blue paper.

'That's my birthday present,' he said. 'It was in the cupboard under the sink. Mum doesn't know I found it. I'm not supposed to have it until next week.'

'What's in it?' asked Bopper.

'Dunno, I haven't opened it.'

Everyone loves a mystery parcel. I could feel three soft lumps when I took it into my hands. Foxy shook it and Bopper sniffed at it, but Murdo's present didn't rattle or smell.

'Careful! I don't want anything to happen to it,' he said.

'It won't,' Foxy assured him. 'Now, everybody put your names on this computer print-out and we'll seal the whole thing up.'

The print-out said:

Dear Stranger from Somewhere in Time,

These things were buried here by

people at the end of the twenty – first

century. If you have time travel,

come back and visit us. We all live in

Mountview Avenue, except Bopper,

Signed: Foxy Ward

Bopper Travolta   Helen Waller

Lorna Lee   Winston Murdoch

We all signed with our full names. The white
time capsule was taped up with our things and
the note inside; then we carried it into the field
behind Murdo's house and buried it.

Chapter Three

NEXT MORNING IT was wet and muddy. It had bucketed all night long. I met Lorna in her new jacket and bright yellow wellies. She was carrying her fancy new camera with all its twiddly bits.

'If it comes I'll ask it to say cheese,' she giggled.

We met Bopper at the corner of Mountview. When the three of us reached Murdo's house, he came to the door looking really miserable.

'Mum's discovered my present is missing,' he said. 'And she won't believe I haven't opened it.'

At that moment Mrs Murdoch appeared and she didn't look at all happy.

'Helen!' she shouted, 'Have you seen a blue parcel? This stupid boy says it's buried somewhere. Who would want to bury a birthday present? The thing will be ruined for goodness sake!'

'It's in a time capsule,' Bopper piped up.

'It's in a what?'

'A time capsule. We've got everything. Bread, tin-opener, Frisbee, oven glove . . .'

'And my oven glove? You buried that, too!'

'We'll get it for you now, Mrs Murdoch,' I said quickly. 'Everything is nicely wrapped up in a polystyrene box.'

That seemed to do the trick. While his mum stood there wondering, Murdo sneaked past with his coat on. Off we went, picking up a spade from Murdo's garage on the way.

Foxy Ward was already there, standing under an arch of hawthorn at the gloomy edge of the wood. We formed a circle as Murdo slowly began to dig.

'Get a move on, Murdo,' said Bopper. 'I want to see if they got the message.'

'I'm not putting a spade through my birthday present, so you'll have to wait,' Murdo snapped.

But the white box did not appear. As the hole in the ground grew wide and deep, I knew it had vanished. Along with my mother's anti-wrinkle cream. And the mystery parcel. And Bopper's shoe. A crazy thought went through my mind. They'll think people of our time have only got one leg!

In a hurry now, Murdo scooped out more soil – and in the middle of his spade was a small metal box.

I wouldn't have dared to touch it, but Bopper, who doesn't have nerves, snatched it up and prised open the lid. Inside was a small, flat object.

'They've returned our message!' whispered Foxy.

We were looking at a tape cassette.

Chapter Four

WHAT WE NEEDED now was a tape recorder. Foxy said he had one in his kitchen, so naturally there was a mad dash for his house.

His mum and dad were washing the car in the drive. They looked up as we flashed by.

'Where are you going?' asked Mrs Ward.

'Kitchen. Gotta use the tape recorder, Mum.'

'Message from the future!' Bopper added breathlessly.

In went the cassette. Clunk, click, press. The little wheels began to turn and all you could hear was heavy breathing. Ours.

Then: 'Yigs vur piggling tardly over vims dee plaaks.'

'French!' howled Bopper.

'Shh!' said Foxy.

'Earthlings of long ago – we greet you. This is Morlag Kim, Great Lord of Time and the Many Worlds. Your gifts have pleased me.'

Jeepers! I looked at Lorna and she was sucking a strand of hair. Foxy was eating his nails.

'Where's my birthday present?' Murdo suddenly shouted.

'Shh!' Foxy hissed again.

'I, Morlag Kim, have created a time gate for you near the place where you left your gifts. Be there at three o'clock and I will show you … the *future*.'

The message ended. I examined the cassette suspiciously. If this was sent from the future, why were they using a cassette made in Japan?

'Easy,' said Foxy. 'They have to send us something we can use in our own time. If we were sending a message back to the olden days we wouldn't send this cassette. They wouldn't know what it was. We'd send a letter written on stone.'

'Where's my present?' Murdo said again.

'Gone,' said Bopper. 'It's in the future with my shoe. Your mum'll understand, Murdo, don't worry.'

Just then Mr Ward came in, and we decided it was time to go. He gave us a friendly wink, and that was when the truth hit me like a plank.

He knew what was going on! Foxy's dad was
Morlag Kim.

'Of course he is, Lorna,' I said to her at the
gate. 'I bet Foxy put him up to it.'

'Bopper thinks Morlag Kim is real,' said Lorna.
'So does Murdo.'

'Lorna. Bopper thinks Donald Duck is real
and poor Murdo can't think of anything but
his birthday present. That Foxy is planning
something for this afternoon, you'll see.'

Chapter Five

WHEN WE MET in the field at ten to three Bopper was there, Murdo was there, I was there and Foxy was there.

'Where's Lorna?' Bopper asked me.

'She had to go shopping.'

'She's going to miss this,' said Foxy. 'When you go through a Time Gate you step into a different world. Another time.'

He made it sound natural, like stepping into your bathroom.

'And what happens if this Morlag Kim turns

out to be a real baddie?' I said. 'He might be a monster from the future and he knows who we are and where we live, thanks to you, Alan Ward.'

That was the very moment when the lights started flashing at the edge of the wood - red, yellow, blue, green. They formed a kind of coloured arch over the hawthorn tree. Step through me, they seemed to say, and find yourself in another time. Just like Star Trek.

'It's the Time Gate!' whispered Bopper. And at that moment a creature came out of the bushes.

Our Murdo, who wouldn't say boo to a goose, was taking on Morlag Kim, Great Lord of Time and the Many Worlds. Alone! All for a blue parcel. And he didn't even know what was in it! Suddenly he picked up a stick and flung it towards the shape in the shadows.

Off came the square head (a cardboard box, sprayed silver), and Lorna yelled, 'Cut that out, Murdo! Are you trying to flatten me?'

The fun was almost over now. There was no Stranger from Somewhere in Time – only Lorna in a cardboard suit. There was no Time Gate – only Foxy's flashing lights. His dad had helped him wire up the circuit to a battery. Last night he'd sneaked back, dug up the white box and replaced it with the cassette.

'I fooled you for a while,' he said.

'You did, you did,' Bopper agreed.

'For about ten seconds!' I said. 'Now give me back my mum's anti-wrinkle cream.'

'And my X-ray,' said Lorna. 'That's got great sentimental value.'

Foxy had hidden the white box in the hollow of an old tree. But the lid had come loose during the night. Water had run down the inside of the trunk, filling up the box so that our things were soaked.

What an awful mess! The paper had come off Murdo's present, and three coloured balls could now be seen between a floating nappy and a lump of bloated bread. When Foxy lifted one up, water dribbled out of it like a sponge.

'It was juggling balls!' said Bopper. Murdo's eyes filled up with great big wobbly tears. He bent down, picked up the soggy juggling balls and walked away withoout saying a word.

'Look, we'll have to buy him some new ones,' said Lorna. 'Juggling balls can't cost that much.'

Chapter Six

HOW MUCH DID juggling balls cost?

We hadn't a clue. On the way to the shopping centre I reckoned that they were probably more expensive than a packet of firelighters but cheaper than a whole cooked chicken.

Bopper, Lorna, Foxy and I had managed to scrape up £3.90, but when we got to the shops and saw the price of juggling balls, we were shocked. They were over £10 for a set of three.

'We could just buy one,' said Bopper.

'Don't be stupid!' snapped Lorna. 'Anybody can juggle with one ball. You need three.'

We came out of the shop and sat down by a pool with a fountain. Our new shopping centre is that sort of place – very posh. There are even indoor trees.

Lorna stared gloomily into the pool. Sparkling coins lay on the bottom, as if a pile of loose change had spilled from a giant's pocket.

'Why do people throw money into a pool?' she said.

'For luck,' I guessed.

Bopper peered in, fascinated. 'Whose money is that?'

There was no sign up to warn people off.

'Nobody owns it,' said Bopper. 'That money might belong to anybody, you know.'

It doesn't belong to you, I was about to say – but too late. How anyone could whip off their socks and shoes that quickly is beyond me, but suddenly Bopper's white feet were

flashing through the water like fish.

'Here's fifty pence!' he cried, holding up a coin. And then another. 'Look! There's more. We could buy juggling balls for everybody with the money in here!'

As the money mounted up in Bopper's hand, I began to panic.

'Get out of there, Bopper!' yelled Lorna.

When the man in the uniform appeared, I knew I should run. I couldn't. But Bopper did. He left behind a trail of wet footprints leading to the exit.

'You come back here!' yelled the security man. Turning to us, he grabbed Foxy by the arm. 'Stealing money, were you?'

'We weren't,' said Foxy, white-faced.

I didn't know what to say as I stared up at the important shiny peak on the man's cap. If Morlag Kim had whisked us through his Time Gate at that moment I'd have hugged him.

'Stealing in broad daylight!'

'We weren't stealing,' I said. 'We were trying to stop him, weren't we, Alan?'
Foxy nodded twice, as if testing his neck.

'That boy who ran away doesn't understand about shopping centres,' I added.

'He's stupid!' wailed Lorna.

Wailing was a good idea. The security man let go of Foxy's arm and stepped back. He must have seen in our eyes that we were completely innocent.

'Well don't let me ever see you near that pool ever again.'

Our three heads shook as we mumbled, 'Never.'

Foxy picked up Bopper's shoes and socks, then we hurried outside to freedom.

Chapter Seven

ABOUT HALF-WAY between our shopping centre and Mountview Avenue there is an advertising board where people stick up posters to make you buy things. As we passed this board, it spoke to us.

'Psst! Are you being followed?'

Standing behind it was Bopper, in bare feet. As he put on his socks and shoes, Lorna talked to him loudly and some of the things she said weren't very nice.

But he didn't listen. He never listens.

'Do you think they'll take my toe-prints?' he
said. Foxy fell about laughing at the idea of
people taking toe-prints instead of fingerprints.

'You'll have to give those coins back,
Bopper,' I said. 'And what are you laughing at,
Foxy? This is all your fault. If it wasn't for you
and time travel and strangers from the future
we wouldn't have ruined poor Murdo's present
and nearly got arrested. Now we'll have to go
and say sorry to him and his mum.'

Murdo came to the door. Oddly enough, he
was smiling.

'We're really sorry about your present, Murdo,' I said.

'It's OK. Mum and me blew them dry with the hair drier!'

After all that! They'd blow-dried the things with the hair drier!

Murdo's mum appeared and stared at Bopper's soaking wet trouser bottoms. We told her all about the money in the pool.

'I thought it was anybody's money,' said Bopper. 'Now I don't know what to do.'

'I'm going shopping soon,' Mrs Murdoch said. 'Would you like me to take the money back for you?'

Bopper seemed relieved to empty his pockets and hand over the coins. I guess he didn't feel like a crook on the run any more.

Then we headed home. Personally I was ready for a nice quiet TV programme.

If we ever make a time capsule again I'm putting Alan Ward's brain into it. That'll give them plenty to think about in the far distant future.

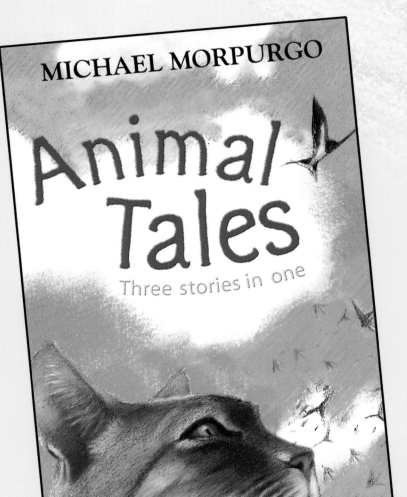

EGMONT PRESS: ETHICAL PUBLISHING

Egmont Press is about turning writers into successful authors and children into passionate readers – producing books that enrich and entertain. As a responsible children's publisher, we go even further, considering the world in which our consumers are growing up.

Safety First
Naturally, all of our books meet legal safety requirements. But we go further than this; every book with play value is tested to the highest standards – if it fails, it's back to the drawing-board.

Made Fairly
We are working to ensure that the workers involved in our supply chain – the people that make our books – are treated with fairness and respect.

Responsible Forestry
We are committed to ensuring all our papers come from environmentally and socially responsible forest sources.

For more information, please visit our website at
www.egmont.co.uk/ethicalpublishing